**For my darling Mitten,
without whom this book would
not have been possible
—Sock**

Atheneum Books for Young Readers · An imprint of Simon & Schuster Children's Publishing Division · 1230 Avenue of the Americas · New York, New York 10020 · Copyright © 2007 by David Gordon · All rights reserved, including the right of reproduction in whole or in part in any form. · Book design by Sonia Chaghatzbanian · The text for this book is set in Bailey ITC. · The illustrations for this book are digitally rendered. · Manufactured in China · 10 9 8 7 6 5 4 3 2 · Library of Congress Cataloging-in-Publication Data · Gordon, David, 1965 Jan. 22– · Smitten / by David Gordon.—1st ed. · p. cm. · Summary: Lost and alone, a sock and a mitten team up to help each other find their other halves. · ISBN-13: 978-1-4169-2440-1 · ISBN-10: 1-4169-2440-X · [1. Mittens—Fiction. 2. Socks—Fiction. 3. Friendship—Fiction.] I. Title. · PZ7.G6547 Sm 2006 · [E]—dc22 · 2005032040

written and illustrated by **david gordon**
based on an original concept by **susan siegel**

tten

new york london toronto sydney

atheneum books for young readers

One cold afternoon, a mitten sat atop a fence post. "Sir!" Mitten called out.

A man bustled by with a basket overflowing with laundry.

"Something is falling out of your . . . !"

And there, on the ground,
lay a single sock.

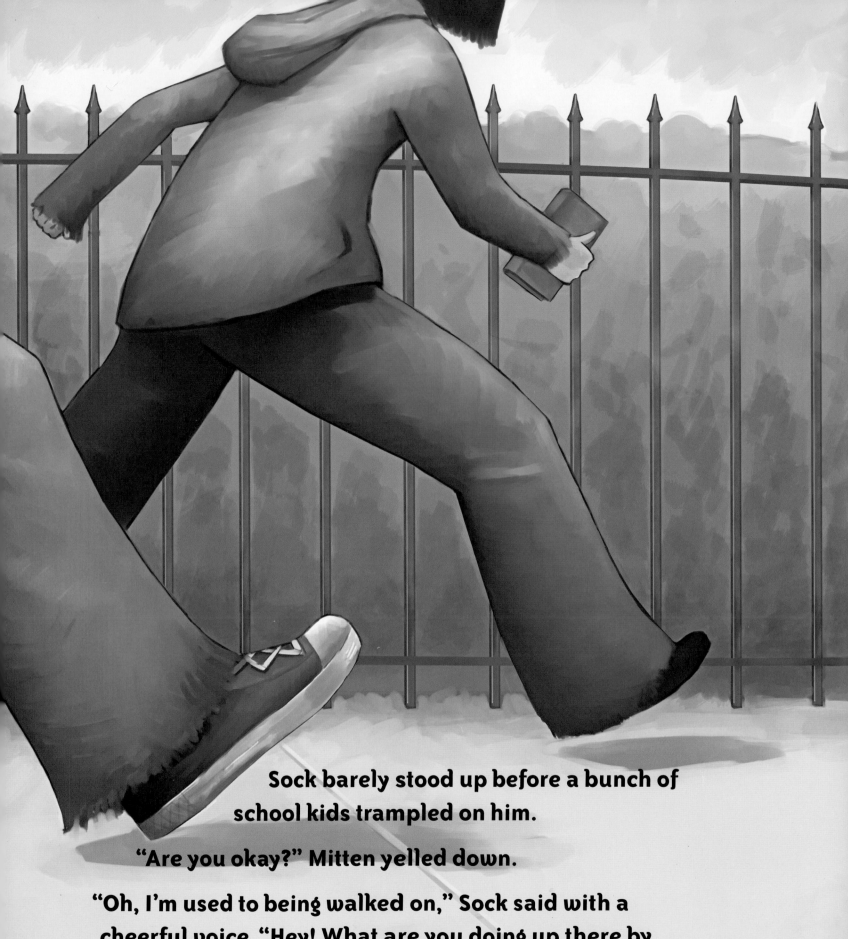

Sock barely stood up before a bunch of school kids trampled on him.

"Are you okay?" Mitten yelled down.

"Oh, I'm used to being walked on," Sock said with a cheerful voice. "Hey! What are you doing up there by yourself?"

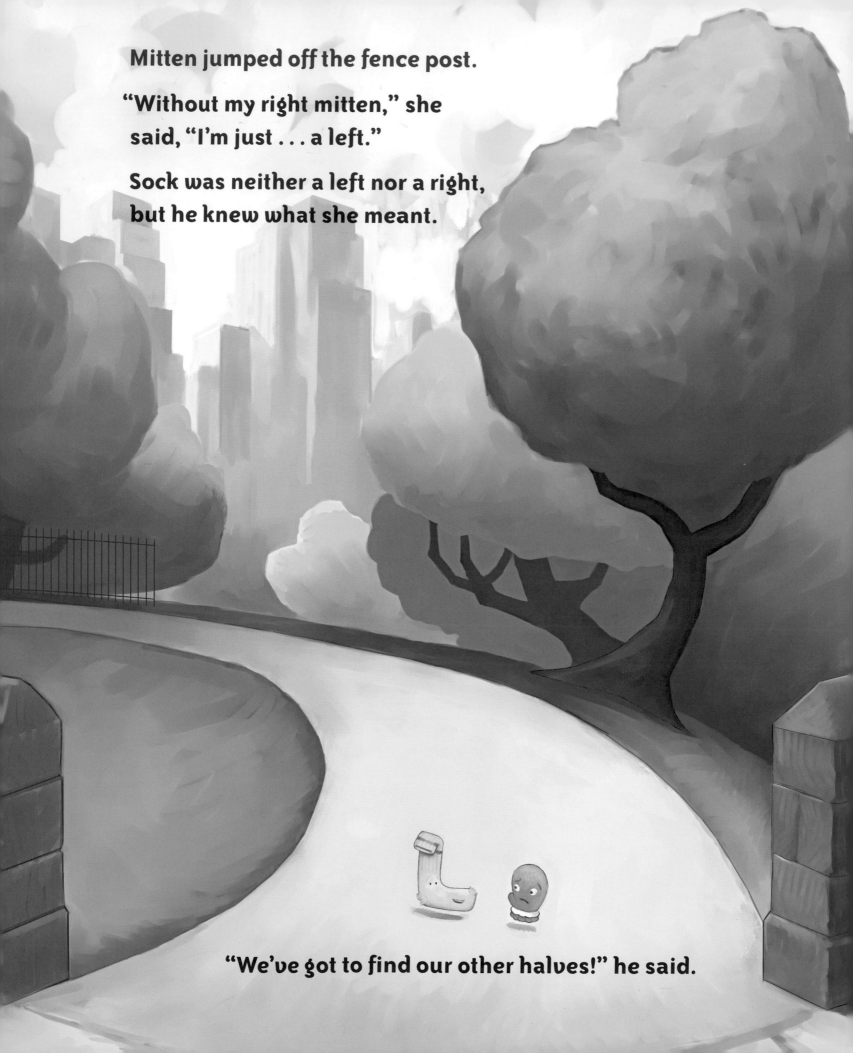

Mitten jumped off the fence post.

"Without my right mitten," she said, "I'm just . . . a left."

Sock was neither a left nor a right, but he knew what she meant.

"We've got to find our other halves!" he said.

As they set off through the park,
Mitten covered her nose.

"What's wrong?" Sock asked.

"I hate to break this to you," said Mitten, "but you don't smell so good."

All of a sudden
Mitten was caught,
flipped, and flung
through the air.

She landed in the trash.

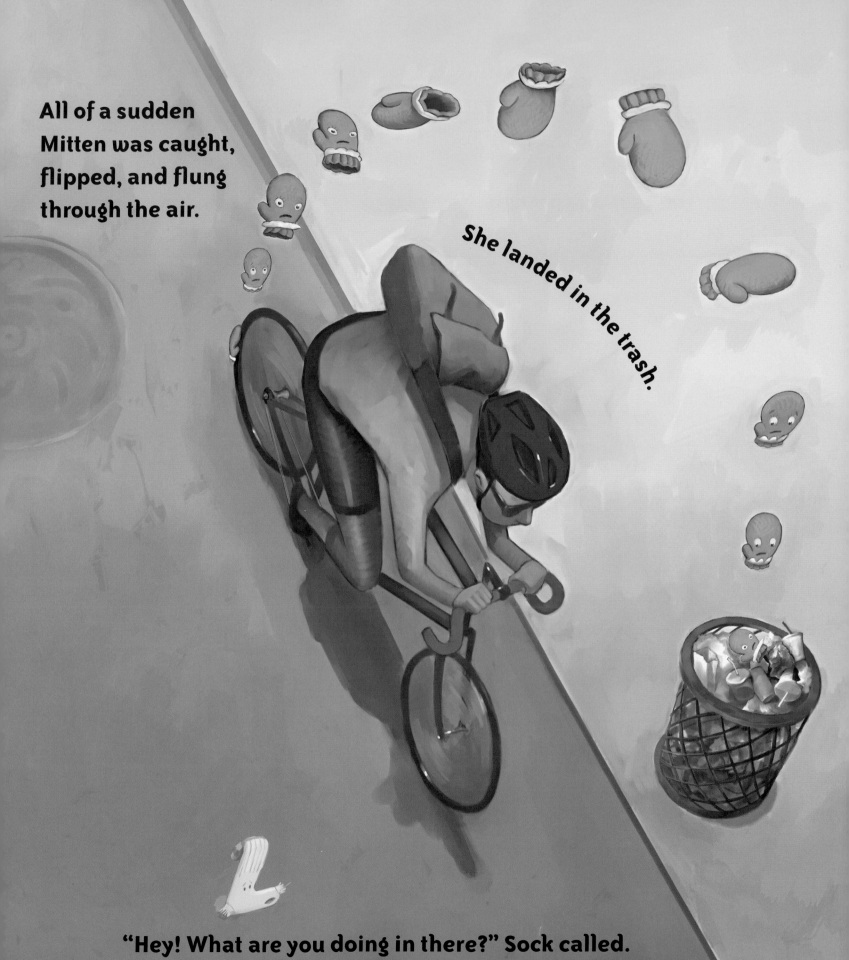

"Hey! What are you doing in there?" Sock called.

Sock pushed and pushed until
the garbage can fell over.

Mitten tumbled out, brushed herself off, and grumbled.

Sock wrinkled his nose.
"Now who doesn't smell so good?"

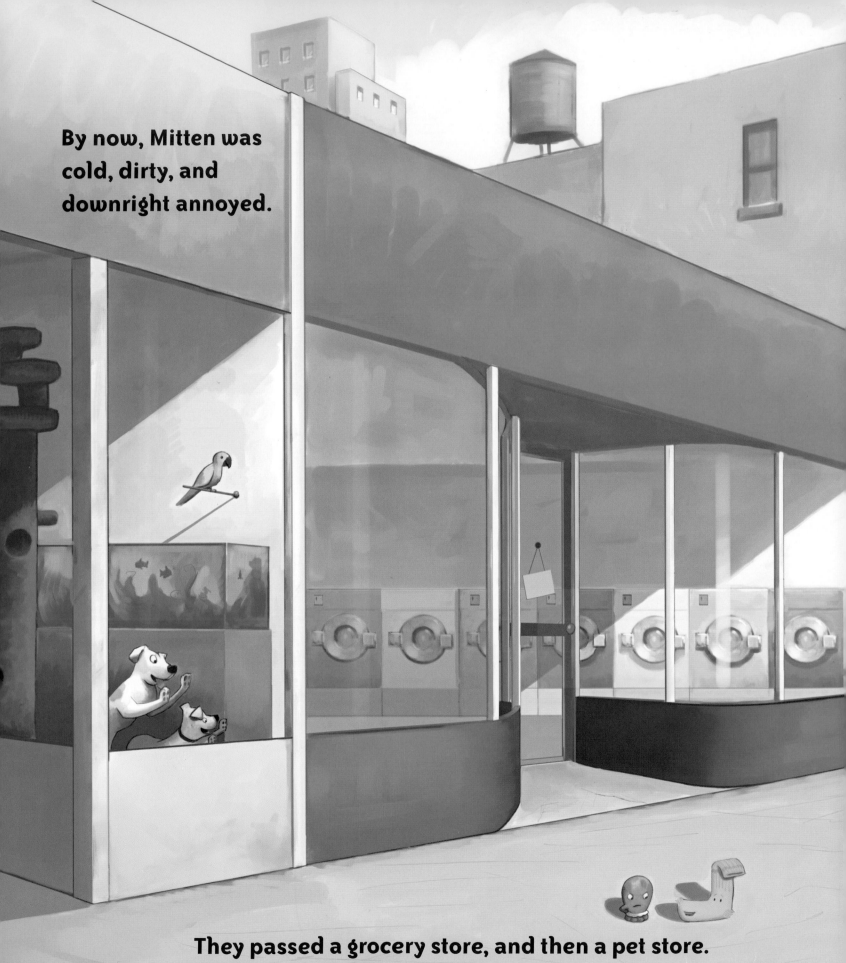

By now, Mitten was cold, dirty, and downright annoyed.

They passed a grocery store, and then a pet store.
Sock stopped in front of a Laundromat.

It was closed, but he had an idea.
"Let's sneak in and get clean!"

Mitten shrugged and followed.

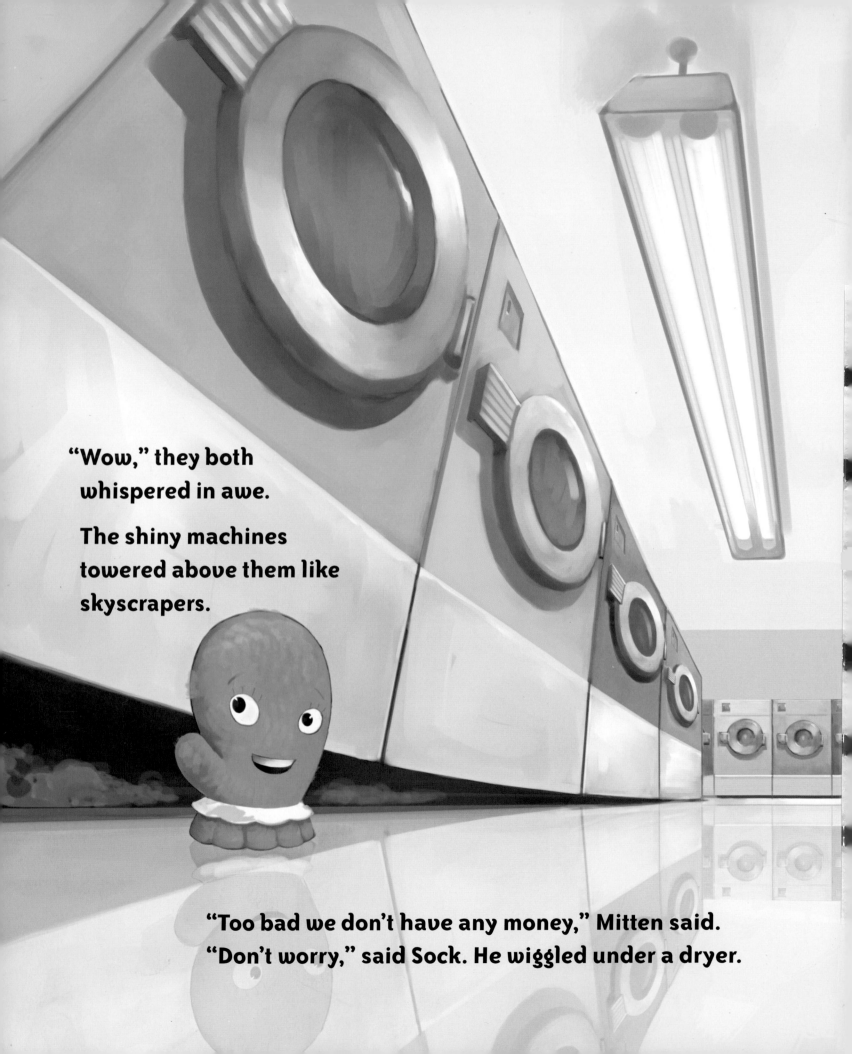

"Wow," they both whispered in awe.

The shiny machines towered above them like skyscrapers.

"Too bad we don't have any money," Mitten said.

"Don't worry," said Sock. He wiggled under a dryer.

Four quarters shot out. Sock emerged, smiling,
and covered with lint. Mitten couldn't help but giggle.

Even Mitten had to admit it looked pretty fun. She tested the water, then eased herself into the warm, soapy suds.

The two played, splashing each other until –

ding! –

the wash cycle was done.

"We'd better get dry," Mitten said,
and she put a quarter in the dryer.

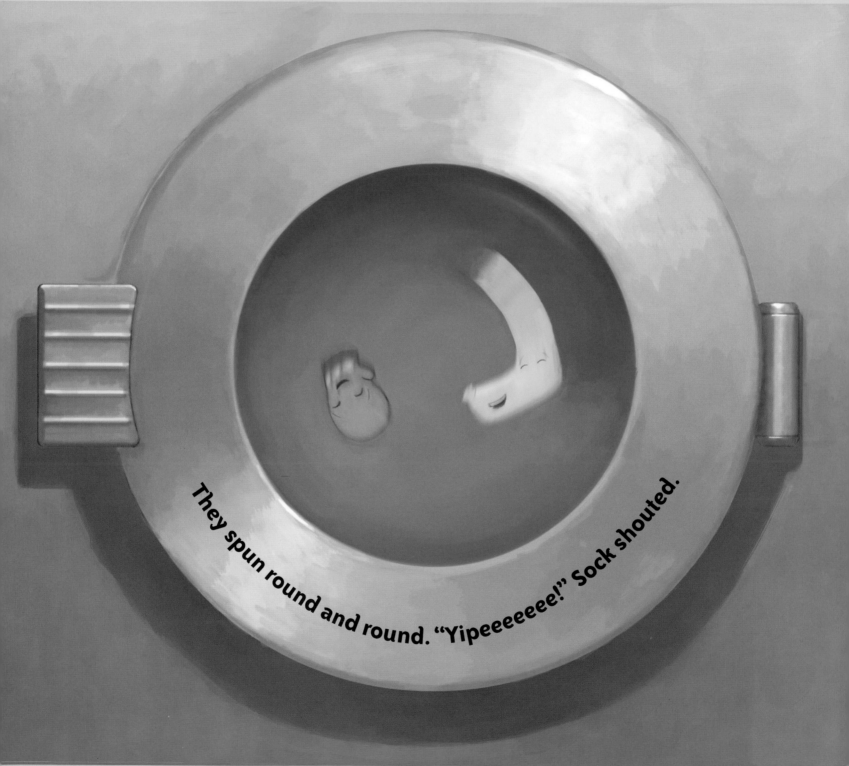

They spun round and round. "Yipeeeeeee!" Sock shouted.

But when Sock stumbled out, he was not only very dizzy,
he had shrunk small enough to fit on a baby doll!

"You should have told me you were wool,"
Mitten muttered.

They made their way out to the sidewalk.
Sock was so tiny that he fell behind.

Suddenly two dogs jumped out from the corner and grabbed him. They tugged and pulled and **stretched** Sock to ten times his size!

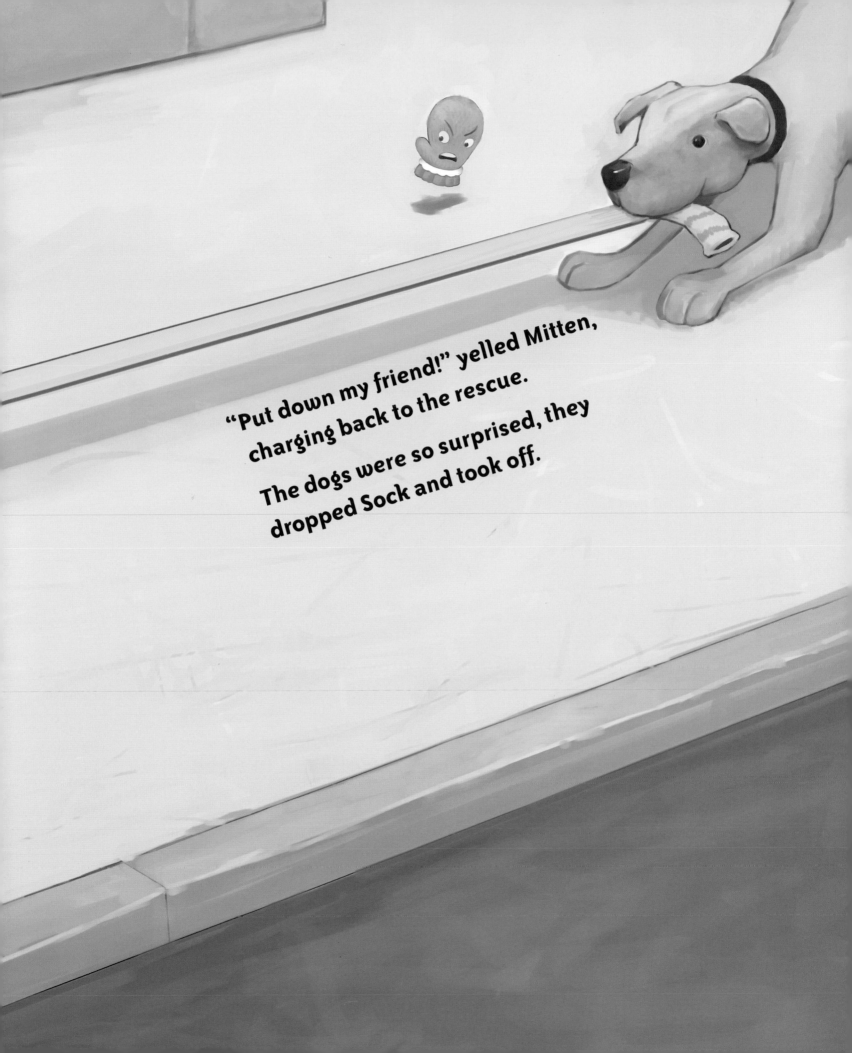

"Put down my friend!" yelled Mitten, charging back to the rescue.

The dogs were so surprised, they dropped Sock and took off.

"I don't feel so good,"
Sock moaned.

"What would you do without me?" Mitten sighed,
and threw him over her shoulder.

Mitten couldn't see where she was going
and walked over a metal grate.

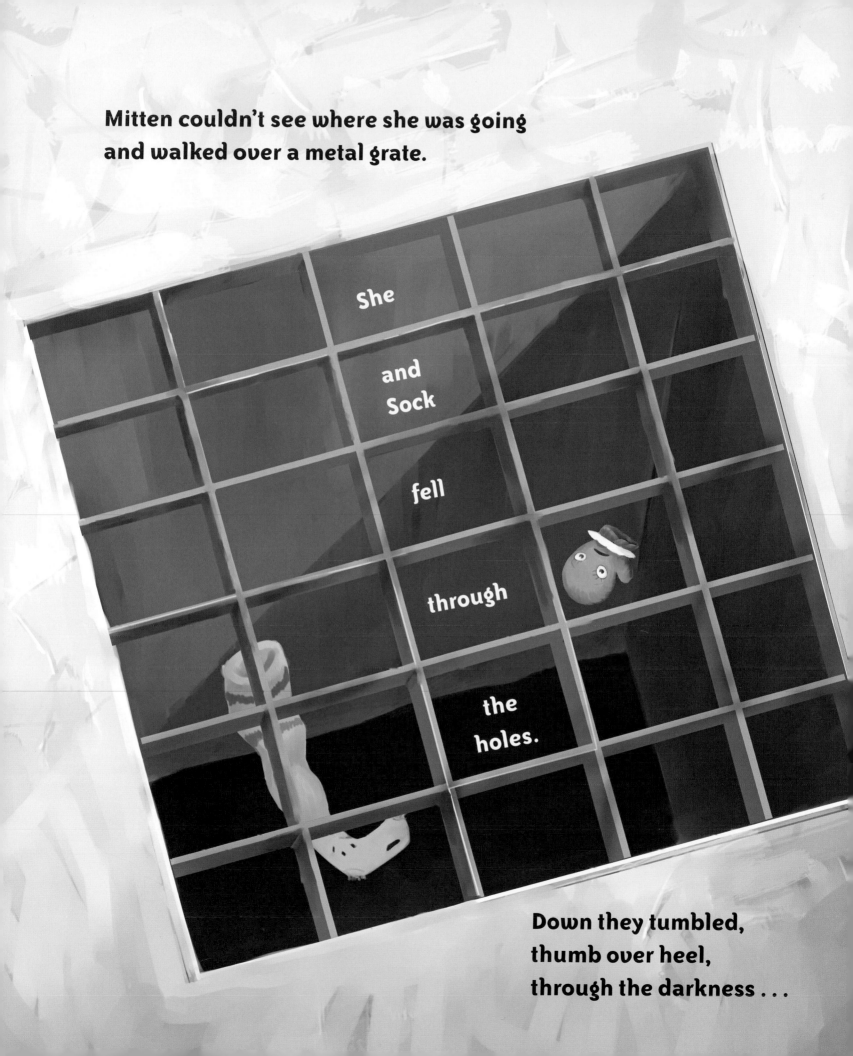

She

and
Sock

fell

through

the
holes.

Down they tumbled,
thumb over heel,
through the darkness . . .

. . . and landed on the subway tracks!

Mitten started to cry. "Now I'll never find my other half!"

"Don't worry, Mitten, we'll be all right," Sock said.

"Oh, no, we won't!" Mitten shouted, pointing at the giant lights bearing down on them.

The train zoomed over them, and one of Mitten's threads got caught on the undercarriage.

She unraveled into one very, very long piece of yarn.

"I don't feel so good,"
Mitten said.

"Don't worry, Mitten, I'm right here," said Sock.
He gently gathered her up into a ball and hopped up the subway stairs.

After a lot of searching,
Sock finally found a knitting store
and snuck in. He grabbed a set of knitting
needles and a good how-to book.

"I'll fix you right up, Mitten."

"This will never work."
Mitten groaned.

But Sock kept knitting through the night
to put his friend back together.

The sun was rising by the time Mitten saw her reflection in a hub cap.

Sock wasn't the best knitter in the world, but despite all her new lumps and bumps, she still looked like a mitten.

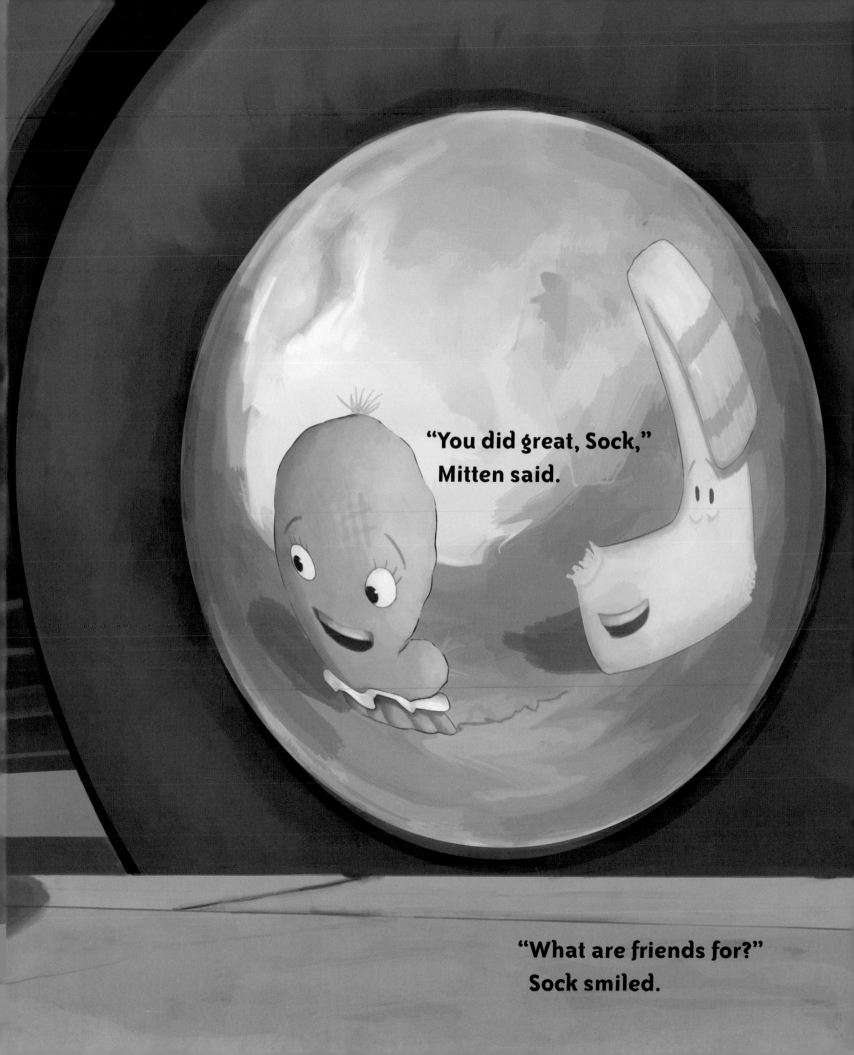

They walked up to a department store window and looked inside. Every sock, mitten, and glove had a match. They all looked so happy, but that's when Mitten realized something.

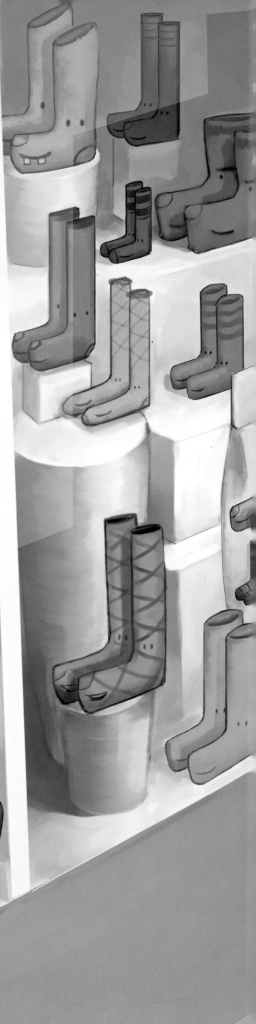

"After everything we've been through,
I think we make the *perfect* pair."

The two friends hugged, and from then on they were . . .

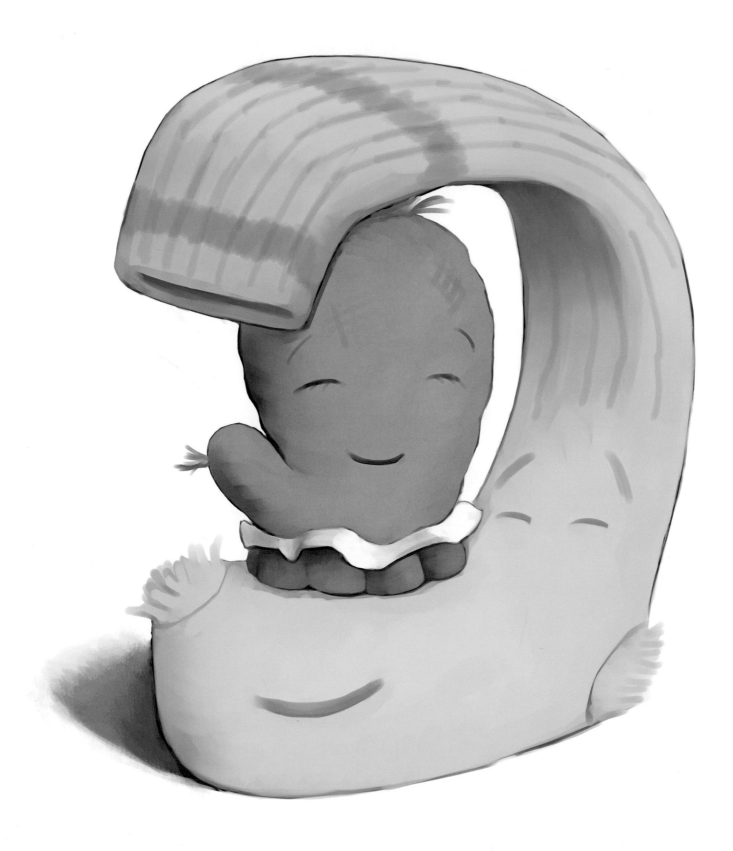

smitten.

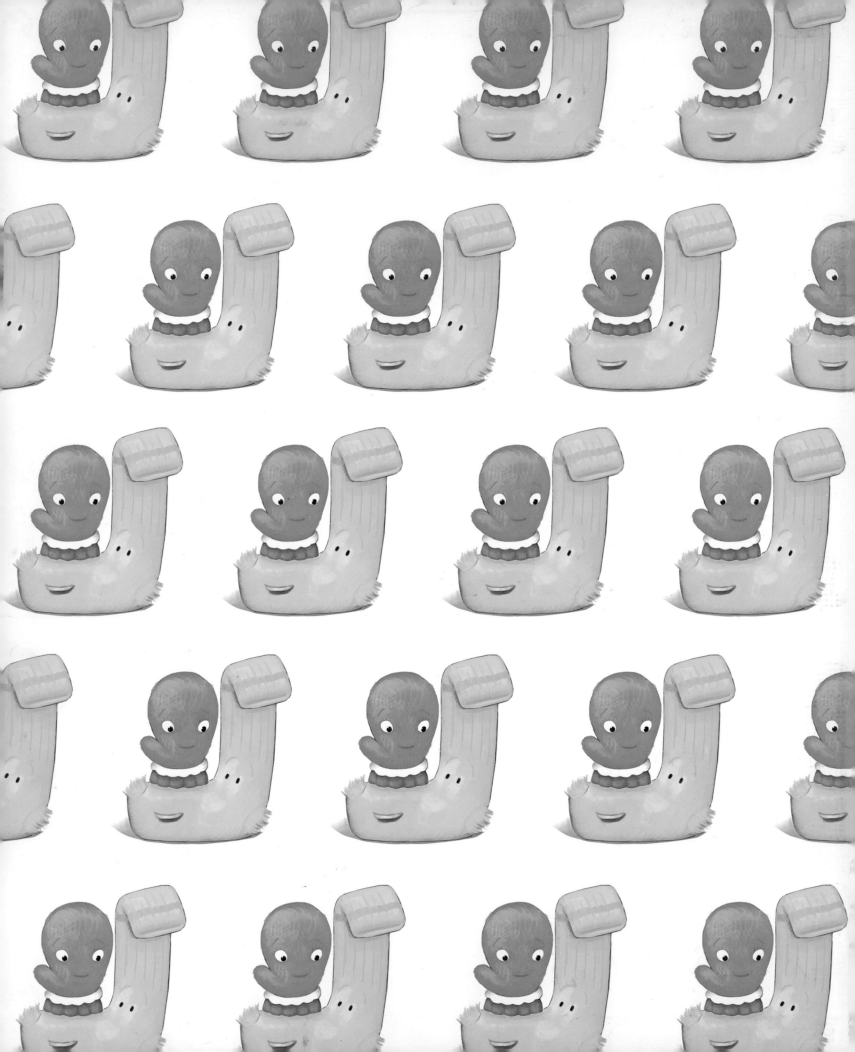